Meerkats

Laura Marsh

NATIONAL
GEOGRAPHIC

Washington, D.C.

For Matthew and Eliza — L. F. M.

The publisher and author gratefully acknowledge the expert review of this book by Peter Santema of the University of Cambridge and the Kalahari Meerkat Project.

Copyright © 2013 National Geographic Society
Published by the National Geographic Society, Washington, D.C. 20036. All rights reserved. Reproduction in whole or in part without written permission of the publisher is prohibited.

ISBN: 978-1-4263-1574-9

Book design by YAY! Design

Printed in the United States of America
13/WOR/1

Table of Contents

What Are They?

They have fun, just like you.
They work, play and rest, too.

They dig in the sand
and lie in the sun.
Most often you'll find
more than one!

What are they? Meerkats!

All About Meerkats

Meerkats are funny to look at. Sometimes they stand on their back legs. Their paws hang down in front.

Meerkats belong to the mongoose family. They live in the desert. It is hot and dry there.

Yellow mongoose

Wild Word

MONGOOSE: A furry animal with a long body and tail. It lives in Africa and Asia.

Terrific Tunnels

A meerkat's home is under the ground. It is called a burrow.

Long tunnels lead to rooms. Meerkats sleep in the burrow at night.

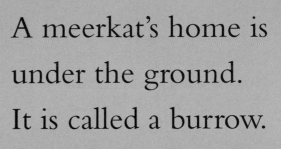

Wild Word

BURROW: A hole or tunnel that an animal digs to use as a home.

On the Menu

Meerkats eat many things. Their favourite foods are beetles and scorpions (SKOR–pee–uns). They like lizards and grubs, too.

Scorpion

Beetle

Lizard

Grubs

How do meerkats find most of their food? They dig for it!

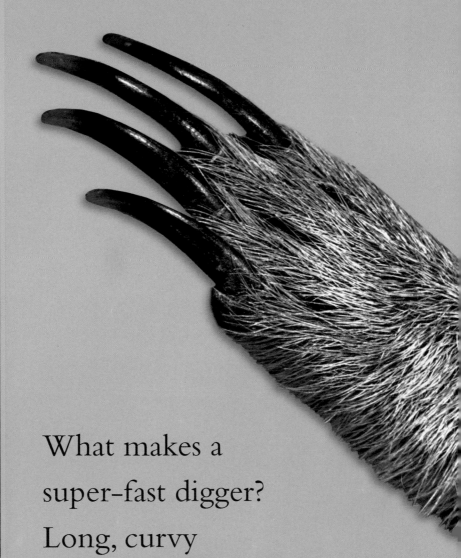

What makes a super-fast digger? Long, curvy claws and four digging paws.

Big Family

Meerkats live in a big group.
A few families live all together.
The group is called a mob.

Meerkats work and rest together.
They also play and sleep together.

A Job to Do

Every meerkat has
a job. Each job helps
the group.

Babysitter

Babysitters

Most of the adults are out hunting. Young meerkats need care. So babysitters watch over them.

Babysitters comfort little ones.

Guards

Guards watch for predators (PRED-uh-turs). They stand on a hill, rock or tree.

Wild Word

PREDATOR: An animal that hunts and eats other animals.

The guards make a loud peeping sound. This warns the others. Look out!

Teachers

Teachers show young meerkats
how to find a meal. They show
them how to eat it, too.

Feeders

Babies need milk. Mothers and other females in the mob feed the babies. The feeders take turns.

A female feeds young meerkats.

7 Cool Facts About Meerkats

1 Meerkats sometimes share their homes with yellow mongooses (above).

2 Meerkats have great noses! They can smell food that's under the sand.

3 Meerkats like to snuggle. It keeps them warm. And they like to stick together.

4

Meerkats lie in the sun
to warm up.

5

A meerkat can dig
hundreds of holes in
one morning!

6

A meerkat burrow usually
has about 15
rooms.

7

A meerkat is about the
size of a squirrel.

Pups

Meerkat babies are called pups. They are born with their eyes closed.

The pups grow fast! They run and dig. Soon the pups will be all grown up.

Staying Safe

Meerkats know what to do when a predator arrives. Sometimes, they stand together. They show their teeth and hiss. This might scare off the predator.

Other times, meerkats just run. They hide in a bolt hole.

Wild Word

BOLT HOLE: A hole in the ground where meerkats run to hide from danger. It's wide enough to fit many meerkats at once.

Meerkats are fun to watch.
But what's extra special
about them?

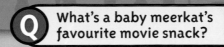

Meerkats help each other!
Sticking together keeps them safe.

What in the World?

These pictures are up-close views of things in a meerkat's world. Use the hints to figure out what's in the pictures. Answers are at the bottom of page 31.

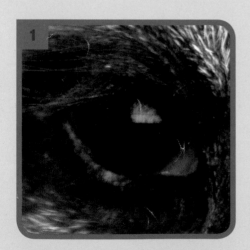

HINT: Meerkats have black circles around these.

HINT: An animal with bumpy skin that meerkats like to eat.

WORD BANK

| Claws | Eye | Beetle | Fur | Lizard | Nose |

HINT: These help meerkats make holes.

HINT: Hair that covers an animal.

HINT: A favourite snack for meerkats.

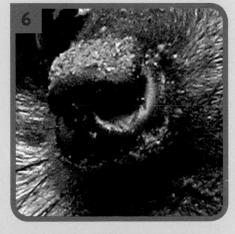

HINT: Meerkats have one. So do you.

Answers: 1. Eye, 2. Lizard, 3. Claws, 4. Fur, 5. Beetle, 6. Nose.

BOLT HOLE: A hole in the ground where meerkats run to hide from danger. It's wide enough to fit many meerkats at once.

BURROW: A hole or tunnel that an animal digs to use as a home.

MONGOOSE: A furry animal with a long body and tail. It lives in Africa and Asia.

PREDATOR: An animal that hunts and eats other animals.